To Harriet, Ted and Eleanor

Library of Congress Cataloging-in-Publication Data

Dunbar, Joyce.
    Why is the sky up? / Joyce Dunbar ; illustrated by James Dunbar. —
1st American ed.
        p.   cm.
    "Originally published in Great Britain in 1991 by J. M. Dent & Sons
Ltd." — T. p. verso.
    Summary: As he is being put to bed a child asks his father
a series of challenging questions about the physical reality of
our planet.
    ISBN 0-395-57580-X
    [1. Nature — Fiction.]   I. Dunbar, James, ill.   II. Title.   .
PZ7.D8944Wh   1991   90-48034
[E] — dc20   CIP
                           AC

Text copyright © 1991 by Joyce Dunbar
Illustrations copyright © 1991 by James Dunbar
First American edition 1991
Originally published in Great Britain in 1991 by J. M. Dent & Sons Ltd.

Printed in Italy
10   9   8   7   6   5   4   3   2   1

WHY IS THE SKY UP?

Joyce and James Dunbar

Houghton Mifflin Company

Boston 1991

"Dad, why is the day light?"

"So that we know when to get up. So that we can see. If the day were dark we'd get our clothes all mixed up."

"Dad, why are we the right way up?"

"If we were upside down, it would be very difficult to eat breakfast. The food would all fall to the floor."

"Dad, why is the park outside?"

"Because the park is too big to be inside. Trees don't grow in living rooms. You can't have a lake indoors."

"Dad, why is the sky up?"

"Because if the sky were down we would walk on it and trample all over it. It's so soft we might fall through."

"Dad, why does the sun shine?"

"The sun shines to make us warm. It shines to show our shadows. Then we know what shape we are. Just think what would happen if the shapes got mixed up."

"Dad, why do the clouds move?"

"The wind blows them along. If we were as light as the clouds the wind would blow us along too."

"Dad, why does the rain fall in drops?"

"Because if the rain fell all at once we'd get very wet. We might have to swim all the way home."

"Dad, why can't I see the stars in the daytime?"

"Perhaps if you could see them you'd try
to catch them and take them home.
Then the moon would be all by itself."

"Dad, why is the moon so far away?"

"The moon is far away to make us wonder why. If
the moon were near we might turn it into a parking lot.
Then it wouldn't be shiny anymore."

"Dad, why is the night dark?"

"So that the world knows when to go to bed, and that means you know too."

"Dad, why is there a world?"

"Because if there were no world there would be
no day, no sky, no sun . . .

no shadows, no stars, no moon . . .
no you, no me, no questions.
Good night now."